The Littlest Pilgrim

Written by
Brandi Dougherty

Illustrated by
Kirsten Richards

Cartwheel
·B·O·O·K·S·®

SCHOLASTIC INC.

New York Toronto London Auckland Sydney Mexico City New Delhi Hong Kong Buenos Aires

For my mom
—B.D.

For Neil, Vic, Bart, and Wendy.
Thanks, guys!
— K.R.

Text copyright © 2008 by Brandi Dougherty.
Illustrations copyright © 2008 by Kirsten Richards.

ISBN-13: 978-0-545-05372-3
ISBN-10: 0-545-05372-2

10 9 8 7   40   10 11 12

Printed in the U.S.A.
First Scholastic printing, October 2008

The Littlest Pilgrim

Mini was a Pilgrim.
She lived with her family in a small village.

There were many Pilgrims in her village,
but Mini was the littlest one.

Even though she was small,
Mini tried to help with the village chores.

One day, Mini decided to be extra helpful.

Mini found her big brother by the house.
He was stacking wood for the winter.
She wanted to help.

"Look, brother," Mini said. "I am helping to make a woodpile."
But Mini's brother was too busy to notice her.

Mini went inside the house and found her big sister. She was mending a dress.

"I am ready to sew," said Mini.
"Sorry, Mini," said her sister, "you are
too little to help with mending.
Go help Mama. I am busy."

So Mini went outside to help her mother.
She was at the oven, baking bread for dinner.

"Look, Mama," said Mini. "I am helping."

But Mini's mother was so busy making bread, she didn't even hear Mini.

Mini went to find her father. Surely he would want some help.
He was getting ready to hunt for food in the forest.

"Sorry, Mini, you are too little for hunting," Mini's father said when he saw her.
"Why don't you go pick some berries for us to eat?"

As Mini walked toward the berry bushes,
she spotted her neighbor.
He was fixing the door to his house.

"I can help ..." Mini started to say.
"Sorry, Mini, this is a big job and
you are too little."

Mini wandered through the village.
She was sad.

Mini just wanted to help, but everyone was too busy to notice.
Or they thought the jobs were too big and Mini was too little.
It wasn't fair.

Mini walked toward the water.
She spotted some boys from her village.
They were fishing.

"Can I help you fish?" Mini asked one of the boys. He laughed. "Sorry, Mini, you are too little for fishing."

Now Mini was very sad.
Why would no one let her help?
Mini knew there had to be something special she could do.

Even if she was little.

Mini started to walk home, and saw some berries along the way.
As she picked them, she heard something rustling in the leaves.
Mini moved closer to get a better look.

There, at the edge of the forest, stood a girl.

And she was little!
Just like Mini.

"Hello," said Mini.
"What's your name?"

The girl stood still and looked at Mini.
She didn't say a word.

Mini remembered the berries she held in her hand. "Do you want one?" she asked.

At first, the girl just stared at Mini.
But soon she began to smile a very big smile.

Mini was too little for many things.
But she was not too little to make a friend.